Crocodile Tears

Pam Scheunemann
Illustrated by Neena Chawla

Consulting Editor, Diane Craig, M.A./Reading Specialist

ABDO
Publishing Company

Published by ABDO Publishing Company, 4940 Viking Drive, Edina, Minnesota 55435.

Printed in the United States.

Credits
Edited by: Pam Price
Curriculum Coordinator: Nancy Tuminelly
Cover and Interior Design and Production: Mighty Media
Photo Credits: Corbis Images, Digital Vision, iStockphoto/Heinri Brink, iStockphoto/Nicola Brown, iStockphoto/Catherine Milton, iStockphoto/John Neuner, iStockphoto/Konrad Steynberg, ShutterStock

Library of Congress Cataloging-in-Publication Data

Scheunemann, Pam, 1955-
    Crocodile tears / Pam Scheunemann; illustrated by Neena Chawla.
        p. cm. -- (Fact & fiction. Critter chronicles)
    Summary: When Rocky Dial joins the other members of the school diving team at the pool, he is afraid they will laugh at his new braces. Alternating pages provide facts about crocodiles.
    ISBN 10 1-59928-436-7 (hardcover)
    ISBN 10 1-59928-437-5 (paperback)

    ISBN 13 978-1-59928-436-1 (hardcover)
    ISBN 13 978-1-59928-437-8 (paperback)
    [1. Crocodiles--Fiction. 2. Self-perception--Fiction. 3. Swimming--Fiction.] I. Chawla, Neena, ill. II. Title. III. Series.

PZ7.S34424Cro 2007
[E]--dc22   2006005333

SandCastle Level: Fluent

SandCastle™ books are created by a professional team of educators, reading specialists, and content developers around five essential components—phonemic awareness, phonics, vocabulary, text comprehension, and fluency—to assist young readers as they develop reading skills and strategies and increase their general knowledge. All books are written, reviewed, and leveled for guided reading, early reading intervention, and Accelerated Reader® programs for use in shared, guided, and independent reading and writing activities to support a balanced approach to literacy instruction. The SandCastle™ series has four levels that correspond to early literacy development. The levels help teachers and parents select appropriate books for young readers.

Emerging Readers	**Beginning Readers**	**Transitional Readers**	**Fluent Readers**
(no flags)	(1 flag)	(2 flags)	(3 flags)

These levels are meant only as a guide. All levels are subject to change.

FACT & FICTION

This series provides early fluent readers the opportunity to develop reading comprehension strategies and increase fluency. These books are appropriate for guided, shared, and independent reading.

FACT The left-hand pages incorporate realistic photographs to enhance readers' understanding of informational text.

FICTION The right-hand pages engage readers with an entertaining, narrative story that is supported by whimsical illustrations.

The Fact and Fiction pages can be read separately to improve comprehension through questioning, predicting, making inferences, and summarizing. They can also be read side-by-side, in spreads, which encourages students to explore and examine different writing styles.

FACT OR FICTION? This fun quiz helps reinforce students' understanding of what is real and not real.

SPEED READ The text-only version of each section includes word-count rulers for fluency practice and assessment.

GLOSSARY Higher-level vocabulary and concepts are defined in the glossary.

SandCastle™ would like to hear from you.

Tell us your stories about reading this book. What was your favorite page? Was there something hard that you needed help with? Share the ups and downs of learning to read. To get posted on the ABDO Publishing Company Web site, send us an e-mail at:

sandcastle@abdopublishing.com

Crocodiles protect their eggs and stay with their young until the babies are a year or two old.

Rocky Dial loves to swim. As he heads off to the pool, his mom shouts out after him, "Rocky, did you remember your nose plugs, ear plugs, and goggles?"

"Yes, Mother," Rocky shouts into the wind behind him as he scurries off.

5

Unlike alligators, the fourth tooth on each side of a crocodile's lower jaw shows when its mouth is closed.

Rocky and his cousins Reed Dial and Ali Gator are on the school swimming team. Reed says, "Hi, Rocky." Rocky returns the greeting but doesn't smile. He just got braces and doesn't want to be laughed at.

7

Crocodiles' rough, dark skin helps them blend in with logs floating in the water.

As Rocky puts on the ear and nose plugs, he asks Reed, "Where is Ali?"

"Over by the logs," Reed replies.

Instead of outer ears, crocodiles have special slits in their heads that lead to inner ears. These slits close when they go underwater.

But Rocky just hears muffled words. "Where?" he asks again. Reed repeats his answer. Rocky still doesn't hear him and shouts, "What?"

11

Crocodiles' eyes are on top of their heads. This allows them to swim at the water's surface and watch for food.

Reed points to where Ali is sitting. Rocky nods and puts on his goggles. He thinks to himself, "I look like a frog in these!"

13

A transparent third eyelid protects crocodiles' eyes from water. Tears formed under this eyelid keep their eyes clean and moist.

Rocky dives in and swims over to where Ali is basking in the sun. Ali sees Rocky in the pool and says, "Cool braces! Your teeth look really sharp with those on." Everyone laughs at the pun.

15

A crocodile can use its powerful tail to leap out of the water to catch flying prey.

As Rocky jumps out of the pool,
he hears something about braces,
and then hears everyone laughing.
He bursts into tears and runs away.

On land, crocodiles can crawl on their bellies, walk, or run. Smaller crocodiles can even gallop for short distances.

Ali sees Rocky and gallops after him. "Hey, Rocky!" Ali shouts. "Pull out those ear plugs! We're not laughing at you! We were just saying how sharp your teeth look in braces. Get it? Sharp?"

Rocky finally flashes a toothy smile. "Really?" he asks. "I guess it would help if I could hear what you were saying. Thanks for the compliment!"

19

FACT or FicTion?

Read each statement below. Then decide whether it's from the FACT section or the FicTion section!

  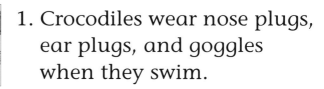

1. Crocodiles wear nose plugs, ear plugs, and goggles when they swim.

2. Crocodiles join swimming teams.

3. Crocodiles' eyes are on top of their heads.

4. Crocodiles have a transparent third eyelid.

ANSWERS
1. fiction 2. fiction 3. fact 4. fact

Crocodiles protect their eggs and stay with their young until the babies are a year or two old.

Unlike alligators, the fourth tooth on each side of a crocodile's lower jaw shows when its mouth is closed.

Crocodiles' rough, dark skin helps them blend in with logs floating in the water.

Instead of outer ears, crocodiles have special slits in their heads that lead to inner ears. These slits close when they go underwater.

Crocodiles' eyes are on top of their heads. This allows them to swim at the water's surface and watch for food.

A transparent third eyelid protects crocodiles' eyes from water. Tears formed under this eyelid keep their eyes clean and moist.

A crocodile can use its powerful tail to leap out of the water to catch flying prey.

On land, crocodiles can crawl on their bellies, walk, or run. Smaller crocodiles can even gallop for short distances.

8
18
28
37
45
51
60
70
74
84
95
102
111
115
126
132
141
150
151

Rocky Dial loves to swim. As he heads off to 10
the pool, his mom shouts out after him, "Rocky, 19
did you remember your nose plugs, ear plugs, 27
and goggles?" 29

"Yes, Mother," Rocky shouts into the wind 36
behind him as he scurries off. 42

Rocky and his cousins Reed Dial and Ali Gator 51
are on the school swimming team. Reed says, 59
"Hi, Rocky." Rocky returns the greeting but doesn't 67
smile. He just got braces and doesn't want to be 77
laughed at. 79

As Rocky puts on the ear and nose plugs, he 89
asks Reed, "Where is Ali?" 94

"Over by the logs," Reed replies. 100

But Rocky just hears muffled words. "Where?" 107
he asks again. Reed repeats his answer. Rocky 115
still doesn't hear him and shouts, "What?" 122

Reed points to where Ali is sitting. Rocky nods
and puts on his goggles. He thinks to himself, "I
look like a frog in these!"

Rocky dives in and swims over to where Ali is
basking in the sun. Ali sees Rocky in the pool and
says, "Cool braces! Your teeth look really sharp with
those on." Everyone laughs at the pun.

As Rocky jumps out of the pool, he hears
something about braces, and then hears everyone
laughing. He bursts into tears and runs away.

Ali sees Rocky and gallops after him. "Hey,
Rocky!" Ali shouts. "Pull out those ear plugs! We're
not laughing at you! We were just saying how
sharp your teeth look in braces. Get it? Sharp?"

Rocky finally flashes a toothy smile. "Really?" he
asks. "I guess it would help if I could hear what you
were saying. Thanks for the compliment!"

GLOSSARY

bask. to enjoy lying or sitting in the sun

compliment. a comment of praise, respect, or admiration

muffle. to make something more quiet or difficult to hear

pun. a joke based on a word that has more than one meaning or that sounds like another word

scurry. to walk or run using short, quick steps

transparent. clear or able to be seen through

To see a complete list of SandCastle™ books and other nonfiction titles from ABDO Publishing Company, visit www.abdopublishing.com or contact us at: 4940 Viking Drive, Edina, Minnesota 55435 • 1-800-800-1312 • fax: 1-952-831-1632